THE CHRISTMAS PAGEANT

by Elizabeth Winthrop
illustrated by Kathy Wilburn

For Alan Houghton

A GOLDEN BOOK, NEW YORK

Western Publishing Company, Inc., Racine, Wisconsin 53404

It was Christmas Eve.
Snow was falling.
In the park, animals had left
tracks in the snow.
Maggie and her father were
walking to church.
Maggie was going to be an angel
in the Christmas pageant.

"Listen," said Maggie's father. "You can hear people singing."

"I can hear the sheep," said Maggie.

There would be real animals in the pageant.

Maggie and her father went into the back of the church.

Some of the other children were already there.

Maggie put on her long white robe and her silver wings. Her father tied the silver ribbon around her head.

"Here come the animals," a boy said.
Everyone crowded around to pat the sheep.
The donkey looked sleepy. Maggie stroked
his brown coat.

"Quiet, please," said Mrs. Walker, their Sunday school teacher. "The trumpets are playing. It's time to line up. Find your partners."

Shepherds bumped into angels. One king tripped on his robe. The littlest angel began to cry.

Sarah was Maggie's partner. They
squeezed hands and smiled.

The boy who was playing Joseph
led the donkey down the aisle with
Mary riding on the donkey's back.

Maggie heard a voice.
"And she brought forth her firstborn son and laid him in a manger."

"It's our turn soon," Sarah whispered.

The shepherds began to herd the sheep up to the altar. One of the sheep bleated.

"Here we go," Maggie said.

The angels skipped up to the altar.
They stood in a circle, holding hands
and singing.

The three kings were the last ones to march up the aisle. Now all the children were gathered around the manger.

The people in the church stood up.
Together, they sang "Silent Night."

All the kings and shepherds
and angels and animals paraded back
down the aisle to the big church doors.

Maggie's parents found her in the crowd. They each gave her a big hug.

"Merry Christmas, Maggie," said Maggie's mother.

"You were a very special angel," said her father.

3394